Acting Edition

Danny Looks Back
and
The Burning Ship

two plays by
David Rabe

Danny Looks Back Copyright © 2024 by David Rabe
The Burning Ship Copyright © 2024 by David Rabe
All Rights Reserved

DANNY LOOKS BACK AND THE BURNING SHIP is fully protected under the copyright laws of the United States of America, the British Commonwealth, including Canada, and all member countries of the Berne Convention for the Protection of Literary and Artistic Works, the Universal Copyright Convention, and/or the World Trade Organization conforming to the Agreement on Trade Related Aspects of Intellectual Property Rights. All rights, including professional and amateur stage productions, recitation, lecturing, public reading, motion picture, radio broadcasting, television, online/digital production, and the rights of translation into foreign languages are strictly reserved.

ISBN 978-0-573-71088-9

www.concordtheatricals.com
www.concordtheatricals.co.uk

FOR PRODUCTION INQUIRIES

UNITED STATES AND CANADA
info@concordtheatricals.com
1-866-979-0447

UNITED KINGDOM AND EUROPE
licensing@concordtheatricals.co.uk
020-7054-7298

Each title is subject to availability from Concord Theatricals Corp., depending upon country of performance. Please be aware that *DANNY LOOKS BACK* and *THE BURNING SHIP* may not be licensed by Concord Theatricals Corp. in your territory. Professional and amateur producers should contact the nearest Concord Theatricals Corp. office or licensing partner to verify availability.

CAUTION: Professional and amateur producers are hereby warned that *DANNY LOOKS BACK* and *THE BURNING SHIP* are subject to a licensing fee. The purchase, renting, lending or use of this book does not constitute a license to perform this title(s), which license must be obtained from Concord Theatricals Corp. prior to any performance. Performance of this title(s) without a license is a violation of federal law and may subject the producer and/or presenter of such performances to civil penalties. Both amateurs and professionals considering a production are strongly advised to apply to the appropriate agent before starting rehearsals, advertising, or booking a theatre. A licensing fee must be paid whether the title(s) is presented for charity or gain and whether or not admission is charged. Professional/Stock licensing fees are quoted upon application to Concord Theatricals Corp.

This work is published by Samuel French, an imprint of Concord Theatricals Corp.

No one shall make any changes in this title(s) for the purpose of production. No part of this book may be reproduced, stored in a retrieval system, scanned, uploaded, or transmitted in any form, by any means, now known or yet to be invented, including mechanical, electronic, digital, photocopying, recording, videotaping, or otherwise, without the prior written permission of the publisher. No one shall share this title(s), or any part of this title(s), through any social media or file hosting websites.

For all inquiries regarding motion picture, television, online/digital and other media rights, please contact Concord Theatricals Corp.

MUSIC AND THIRD-PARTY MATERIALS USE NOTE

Licensees are solely responsible for obtaining formal written permission from copyright owners to use copyrighted music and/or other copyrighted third-party materials (e.g. artworks, logos) in the performance of this play and are strongly cautioned to do so. If no such permission is obtained by the licensee, then the licensee must use only original music and materials that the licensee owns and controls. Licensees are solely responsible and liable for clearances of all third-party copyrighted materials, including without limitation music, and shall indemnify the copyright owners of the play(s) and their licensing agent, Concord Theatricals Corp., against any costs, expenses, losses and liabilities arising from the use of such copyrighted third-party materials by licensees. For music, please contact the appropriate music licensing authority in your territory for the rights to any incidental music.

IMPORTANT BILLING AND CREDIT REQUIREMENTS

If you have obtained performance rights to this title, please refer to your licensing agreement for important billing and credit requirements.

For Deborah Treisman

DANNY LOOKS BACK
or
Things We Worried About When I Was Ten

DANNY LOOKS BACK was first published under the title "Things We Worried About When I Was Ten" in the February 3, 2020, issue of *The New Yorker*.

CHARACTER

DANNY MATZ – A man of a certain age and type, casually dressed.

PRODUCTION NOTE

A production could make use of projection images, offstage sound effect. The literal might serve, as in door slams. The sounds of banging on pots and pans, or of a mob, or of fire. Or there might only be music. There could be props. I'm writing this to indicate that I welcome what a director and actor could explore. On the other hand, the piece might be best served by an expressive, versatile actor working on his own to render the people and events depicted. I will make suggestions at a few places where a prop or sound effect might be useful. But these are examples of what might work, not things that I am certain should be used. Whatever is done, care must be taken not to encroach on the evocative reach of the actor and his personal rendering of the piece.

(A backdrop whose nature and color can be changed to seem like night sky, sun, or perhaps some reflection of mood or emotion. Silence. Music. **DANNY MATZ**, a man of a certain age and type, casually sits in a colorful webbed lawn chair. A wooden box beside him serves as a table. He drinks a beer, and seems in a reverie of not unpleasant memories. He sips his beer and remembers and speaks, and then he looks to the audience as he might a new friend.)*

Things we worried about when I was ten. High on the list was trying not to have the older boys decide to de-pants you and then run your pants up the flagpole, leaving you in your underwear, and maybe bloodied if you'd struggled – not that it helped, because they were bigger and stronger – and your pants flapping way up against the sky over the schoolyard.

They mostly did this to Freddy Bird – nobody knew why, but it happened a lot. It was best to get away from him when they started to get into that mood – their let's-de-pants-somebody mood.

Oh, there's Freddy Bird. You could see them thinking it. You had to slip sideways, not in an obvious way but as if you were drifting for no real reason, or maybe the wind was shoving you and you weren't really paying attention, and, most important, you did not want to meet eyes with them, not one of them. Because they could change

---

* A license to produce *Danny Looks Back* does not include a performance license for any third-party or copyrighted recordings. Licensees should create their own.

their mind in a flash if they noticed you, as they would if you met their eyes, and then they'd think,

Oh, look, there's Danny Matz, let's de-pants him, and before you knew it you'd be trying to get your pants down from high up on the flagpole while everybody laughed, especially Freddy Bird.

Meeting eyes was, generally speaking, worrisome. It could lead anywhere. I'd been on the Kidnickers' porch with the big boys when they were tormenting Devin Sleverding – pushing him and, you know, spitting on him and not letting him off the porch when he tried to go. Fencing him in. And I felt kind of sorry for Devin, but I didn't let it show, and I made sure that I stayed on the big boys' side of the invisible line that separated them from Devin, who was crying and snorting and looking like a trapped pig, which he was, in a sense, and waving his hands around in that girly way he had, his wrists all fluttery and floppy, which he should have just stopped doing, because that was how he'd got into trouble with the big boys to begin with.

That was another thing we worried about, a sort of worry inside a worry: along with not wanting to meet anybody's eyes, we had to make sure that we never started waving our hands around like girls, the way Devin Sleverding did.

So the older boys had formed a circle around him, and, if he tried to break out, they'd push him back into the middle of the ring, and, if he just stood there, hoping they'd get tired or bored and go play baseball or something, well, then one of them would jump at him and shove him so hard that he staggered over into the boys on the other side of the circle, who would shove him back in the direction he'd come from.

That was what was happening when our eyes met.

I was trying to be part of the circle and to look like I belonged with the big boys and thought he deserved it, waving his hands like a girl. Just stop it, I thought. His snot-covered, puffy red face looked shocked and terribly disappointed, as if seeing me act that way was the last straw, as if he'd expected something more from me.

And I don't know where Devin got the stick – this hunk of wood covered in slivers which had probably been left on the Kidnickers' porch after somebody built something – but he had it and he hit me over the head.

I saw stars, staticky, racing stars no bigger than mouse turds. Blood squirted out of my head, and I fell to my knees, and, while everybody was distracted, Devin made his break.

I was crying and crawling, and one of the big boys said, "You better go home."

"O.K.," I said, and left a blood trail spattering the sidewalk where I walked and alongside the apartment building where I lived and on just about every one of the steps I climbed to our door, which entered into the kitchen, where my mom, when she saw me, screamed.

I had to have stitches.

Another thing I worried about was how to make sure that I never had to box Sharon Weber again.

It was my dad's idea. We'd gone down to Red and Ginger Weber's apartment, which was on the ground floor of our two-story, four-apartment building.

I was supposed to box Ron Weber, who was a year older than me, but he wasn't home, so Red offered his daughter, Sharon, as a substitute, and my dad said sure.

Nobody checked with me, and I didn't know what to say anyway – so there I was, facing off against Sharon, who was a year younger than me, but about as tall.

She hit me square in the nose, a surprise blow, and I just stood there.

"C'mon, Dan," my dad said. "Show her what you got."

I wanted to. But I was frozen. I didn't know what I could do – where to hit her.

She was a girl.

I couldn't hit her in the face, because she was pretty and, being a girl, needed to be pretty, and I couldn't hit her in the stomach, because that was where her baby machinery was, and I didn't want to damage that; I couldn't hit her above her stomach, either, because her chest wasn't a boy's chest – she had breasts, and they were important, too, to babies and in other ways that I didn't understand but had heard about.

So I stood there, getting pounded, ducking as best I could, but not too much, because I didn't want to appear cowardly, afraid of a girl, and covering up, not too effectively, for the same reason, while Sharon whaled away on me.

"Dan, c'mon, now," my dad said. "What are you doing? Give her a good one."

I couldn't see my dad, because my eyes were all watery and blurry – not with tears, just water.

I guess it had dawned on Sharon that nothing was coming back at her, so she was windmilling me and side-arming, prancing around and really winding up.

My dad said, "Goddammit, Dan! Give her a smack, for God's sake."

Red was gloating and chattering to Sharon, as if she needed coaching to finish me off. "Use your left. Set him up."

My dad was red-faced, his mouth and eyes squeezed into this painful grimace, the way they'd been when I spilled boiling soup in his lap. He could barely look at me, like it really hurt to look at me.

He grabbed me then, jerked me out the door. Once we were outside, he left me standing at the bottom of the stairs while he stomped up to our apartment.

I ran after him and got to our part of the long second-floor porch we shared with the Stoner family just in time to see him bang the door shut.

I heard him inside saying, "Goddammit to hell. What is wrong with that kid?"

"What happened?" my mom asked.

"I'm sick of it, you know."

"Sick of what?"

"What do you think?"

"I don't know."

"Never mind," he said. "Goddammit to hell."

"Sick of what? At least tell me that."

"Why bother?"

"Because I'm asking. That ought to be enough."

"Him and you, O.K.?"

"Me?" she said. "Me?"

I heard another door slam.

When I opened the apartment door to peek in, I saw that the door to the bathroom, which was alongside the kitchen, was closed.

My mother was wearing a housedress that I'd seen a million times. It buttoned down the front and never had the bottom button buttoned. She had an apron on and a pot holder around the handle of a pot in her hand. Everything smelled of fish.

She looked at me standing in the doorway with the Webers' boxing gloves on.

"What happened?" she asked.

"I was supposed to box Ron Weber, because Dad thought I could beat him, even though he's older, but he wasn't home, so Sharon –"

"Wait, wait. Stop, stop. What more do I have to put up with?"

She grabbed my arm and pulled me into the kitchen.

"What happened? What happened? What happened?" she said too many times. "Carl," she shouted at the bathroom door. "What happened?"

"I'm on the crapper," he said.

"Oh, my God." She walked like a sad, dizzy person to the table, where she sat down real slow, the way a person does when sliding into freezing or scalding-hot water. She put her chin in her hands, but her head was too heavy and it sank to the tabletop, where she closed her eyes.

I stood for a moment, looking down at my hands in the boxing gloves, wondering how I was going to get out of them.

What if I had to pee?

How could I get my zipper down and my weenie out?

I went into the living room, which was only a few steps away, because the apartment was really small.

I sat on the couch. I wished I could go up into the attic. It wasn't very big and had a low, slanted roof, but it felt far away from everything, with all these random objects lying there, as if history had left them behind. One of them was Dobbins, my rocking horse, who had big white scary eyes full of warnings and mysteries to solve, if he could ever get through to me.

But the only way up to the attic was through the bathroom, which was off limits at the moment because my dad was in there on the crapper.

I worked on the laces of the gloves with my teeth, trying to tug them loose enough that I could clamp the gloves between my knees and pull my hands out, and I made some progress, but not enough. So I gave up. I sat for a while and then I lay down on the couch.

Another thing we worried about was that, if it rained and it was night – not late, because then we had to be in bed, but dark already, and wet, the way a good heavy rain left things – and our parents wouldn't let us go out, or wouldn't let us have a flashlight because we'd run the batteries down, then other kids would get all the night crawlers that came up and slithered in the wet grass.

We worried that they would all be snatched up by the kids whose parents weren't home, or who had their own flashlights.

It was strange to me that night crawlers came up at all, because when they were under the dirt they were hidden and safe.

Maybe, though, if they stayed down there after a heavy rain they would drown. I didn't know and couldn't ask them.

The main thing was that they weren't regular worms but night crawlers, big and fat, with shiny, see-through skin, and we could catch them and put them in a can with coffee grounds and then use them as bait or sell them to men who were going fishing but hadn't had time to go out and catch some themselves.

When our parents did let us go, we raced out our doors and, in my case, down the stairs, then walked around sneakily, searching the grass with a flashlight, the beam moving slowly, like the searchlight in a prison movie when prisoners are trying to escape.

When the light struck a night crawler, we had to be quick, because they were very fast and they tried to squirm back into the holes they'd come out of, or were partway out of, and we had to pinch them against the ground with our fingers and then pull them out slowly, being careful not to break them in half.

Because they somehow resisted – they hung on to their holes without any hands.

We could feel the fear in them as they tried to fight back, so tiny compared with us, though we were only kids, and, when we got them out, the way they twisted and writhed about seemed like silent screaming.

It was odd, though, how much they loved the dirt. We all knew that there were awful things down there.

Germs. Maggots.

You could even suffocate if dirt fell on you in a mudslide. We almost felt as if we were saving the night crawlers, dragging them out and feeding them to fish.

It was impossible to figure it all out.

Another thing we worried about was having to move. What if we had to move?

It happened every now and then to people we knew. Their families moved and they had to go with them. A big truck showed up, and men in uniforms took all the things out of the house and put them into the truck.

It had happened to the Ballingers, for example.

"We're moving," Ronnie said.

"Gotta move," his younger brother, Max, said.

And, the next thing we knew, the trucks were there and the men in and out and then the Ballingers were gone. Every one of them.

The house was empty. We could sneak into their yard and peek in the windows and see the big, scary emptiness, so empty it hurt.

And then other people, complete strangers, showed up and went in and started living there, and it was as if the Ballingers had never been there.

Or Jesus. We all worried about Jesus. I know I did. What did he think of me? Did he, in fact, think of me? At Mass, I took the Host into my mouth, and the priest said that it was Jesus, and the nuns also said that it was Jesus, in this little slip of bread, this wafer that melted on my tongue.

You weren't supposed to chew it or swallow it whole, so you waited for it to melt and spread out holiness.

Hands folded, head bowed, eyes closed until you had to see where you were going to get back to your pew, and there was Mary Catherine Michener entering her pew right in front of you, her eyes downcast, a handkerchief on top of her head because she'd forgotten her hat, and her breasts, which had come out of nowhere, it seemed, and stuck out as if they were taking her somewhere, were big, as if to balance the curve of her rear end, which was sticking out in the opposite direction.

Did Jesus know?

He had to, didn't he, melting as he was in my mouth, trying to fill me with piety and goodness while I had this weird feeling about Mary Catherine Michener, who was only a year or two older than me and whom I'd known when she didn't have pointy breasts and a rounded butt, but now she did, and, seeing them, I thought about them, and the next thought was of confession.

Or of being an occasion of sin.

I did not want to be an occasion of sin for the girls in my class, who could go to Hell if they saw me with my shirt off, according to Sister Mary Irma. And so confession again. Father Paul listening on the other side of the wicker window, or Father Thomas, sighing and sad and bored.

Being made an "example of" by Sister Mary Luke, the principal, was another nerve-racking thing that could happen. You could be an example of almost anything, but, whatever it was, you would be a kind of stand-in for everybody who'd committed some serious offense, and so the punishment would be bad enough to make everybody stop doing it, whatever it was.

Or getting sat on by Sister Conrad.

That shouldn't have been a worry, but it was.

And, though it may sound outlandish, we'd all seen it happen to Jackie Rand.

But, then, almost everything happened to Jackie Rand.

Which might have offered a degree of insurance against its ever happening to us, since so much that happened to Jackie didn't happen to anyone else, and yet the fact that it had happened to anyone, even Jackie, and we'd all seen it, was worrisome.

Sister Conrad, for no reason we could understand, had been facing the big pulldown map and trying to drill into our heads the geographic placement of France, Germany, and the British Isles.

This gave Jackie the chance he needed to poke Basil Mellencamp in the back with his pencil, making him squirm and whisper, "Stop it, Jackie."

But Jackie didn't stop, and he was having so much fun that he didn't notice Sister Conrad turning to look at him.

"Jackie!" she barked.

Startled and maybe even scared, he rocked back in his desk as far as he could to get away from Basil, and aimed his most innocent expression at Sister Conrad.

"Stand up," she told him, "and tell us what you think you are doing."

He looked us over, as if wondering if she'd represented our interest correctly, then he turned his attention to his desk, lifting the lid to peek inside.

"Did you hear me? I told you to stand up, Jackie Rand."

He nodded to acknowledge that he'd heard her, and, shrugging in his special way, which we all knew represented his particular form of stubborn confusion, he scratched his head.

Sister Conrad shot toward him. She was round and short, not unlike Jackie, though he was less round and at least a foot shorter.

All of us pivoted to watch, ducking if we were too close to the black-and-white storm that Sister Conrad had become, rosary beads rattling, silver cross flashing and clanking.

She grabbed Jackie by the arm and he yelped, pulling free.

She snatched at his ear, but he sprang into the aisle on the opposite side of his desk, knocking into Judy Carberger, who cowered one row over.

Sister Conrad lunged, and Basil, who was between them, hunched like a soldier fearing death in a movie where bombs fell everywhere.

"You're going to the principal's office!" she shrieked.

We all knew what that meant – it was one step worse than being made an example of. Stinging rulers waited to smack upturned palms, or, if we failed to hold steady and flipped our palms over in search of relief, the punishment found our knuckles with a different, even worse kind of pain.

Sister Conrad and Jackie both bolted for the door.

Somehow – though we all marvelled at the impossibility of it – Sister Conrad got there first.

Jackie had been slowed by the terrible burden of defying authority, which could make anyone sluggish.

"I want to go home," he said. "I want to go home."

The irony of this wish, given what we knew of Jackie's home, shocked us as much as everything else that was going on.

Jackie leaned toward the door as if the moment were normal, and he hoped for permission, but needed to go.

Sister Conrad stayed put, blocking the way.

He reached around her for the doorknob and she shoved him.

I may have been the only person to see a weird hopelessness fill his eyes at that point. I was his friend, perhaps his only friend, so it was fitting that I saw it. And then he lunged at her and grabbed her.

We gasped to see them going sideways and smashing against the blackboard.

Erasers, chalk sticks, and chalk dust exploded.

Almost every boy in the room had battled Jackie at one point or another, so we knew what Sister Conrad was up against.

We gaped, watching her hug him crazily. Her glasses flew off.

Jackie shouted about going home as he fell over backward. She came with him, crashing down on top of him.

They wrestled, and she squirmed into a sitting position right on his stomach, where she bounced several times.

The white cardboard thing around her head had sprung loose, the edge sticking out, the whole black hood so crooked that it half covered her face.

Jackie screamed and wailed under her, as she bounced and shouted for help and Basil ran to get Sister Mary Luke.

Getting into a fight with Jackie Rand was another thing we worried about. Though it was less of a worry for me than for most. Jackie and I lived catercornered from each other across Jefferson Avenue, which was a narrow street, not fancy like a real avenue.

Jackie lived in a house, while I was in an apartment.

He was rough and angry and mean, it was true – a bully. But not to me. I knew how to handle him. I would talk soothingly to him, as if he were a stray dog.

I could even pull him off his victims. His body had a sweaty, gooey sensation of unhappy fat.

Under him, a boy would beg for mercy, but Jackie, alone in his rage, would be far from the regular world.

When I pulled him off, he would continue to flail, at war with ghosts, until, through his hate-filled little eyes, something soft peered out, and, if it was me that he saw, he might sputter some burning explanation and then run home.

As a group, we condemned him, called him names: "Bully! Pig eyes! Fatso!" The beaten boy would screech, "Pick on somebody your own size, you fat slob!" Others would add, "Lard ass! Fatty-Fatty Two-by-Four!"

The fact that Jackie's mother had died when he was four explained his pouty lips and the hurt in his eyes, I thought. Jackie's father seemed to view him as a kind of commodity he'd purchased one night while drunk. The man would whack him at the drop of a hat.

This was even before Jackie's father had failed at business and had to sell the corner grocery store, and before he remarried, hoping for happiness but, according to everybody, making everything worse.

Jackie's stepmom, May, came with her own set of jabs and prods that Jackie had to learn to dodge, along with his father's anger.

All of us were slapped around. Our dads were laborers who worked with their hands. Some built machines; others tore machines apart. Some dug up the earth; others repaired automobiles or hammered houses into shape. Many slaughtered cows and pigs at the meatpacking company.

Living as they did, they relied on their hands, and they used them. Our overworked mothers were also sharp-tempered and as quick with a slap as they were with their fits of coddling. And, after our parents and the nuns were done, we spent a lot of time beating one another up.

Still, Jackie's dad was uncommon. He seemed to mistake Jackie for someone he had a grudge against in a bar.

But then, as our parents told us, Jackie was "hard to handle." He would "try the patience of a saint," and his dad was "quick-triggered" and hardly happy in his second marriage.

As Jackie and I walked around the block, or sat in a foxhole we'd dug on the hill and covered with sumac, these were among the mysteries that we tried to solve.

"Too bad your dad lost his store," I told him.

"He loved my real mom," Jackie said, looking up at the light falling through the leaves.

"May is nice."

"I know she is. She's real nice."

"He loves you, Jackie."

"Sure."

"He just doesn't know how to show it. You gotta try not to make him mad."

"I make everybody mad."

"But he's quick-tempered."

"I'd try the patience of a saint."

More than once, I went home from time spent with Jackie to stare in wonder and gratitude at my living mother and my dad, half asleep in his big chair, listening to a baseball game.

Sometimes in church I would pray for Jackie, so that he could have as good a life as I did.

In daylight, we did our best, but then there was the time spent in bed at night. It was there that I began to suspect that, while there was much that I knew I worried about, there was more that I worried about without actually knowing what it was that worried me – or even that I was worrying – as I slept.

The things with Mr. Stink and Georgie Baxter weren't exactly in this category, but they were close.

Mr. Stink was a kind of hobo, who built a shack on the hill behind our apartment building, and he had that name because he stank.

We kids were told to stay away from him and we did.

He interested me, though, and I looked at him when I could, and sometimes I saw him looking at us. We all saw him walking on the gravel road between the hill and our houses, lugging bags of junk, on the way to his shack.

Then one night I was in our apartment, doing my homework, while Dad was listening to baseball, and my mom was rocking my baby sister in her lap and trying to talk my dad into listening to something else, when this clanking started.

It went clank-clank-clank and stopped.

Then clank-clank-clank again.

"What the hell now?" my dad griped.

It went on and on, and Dad couldn't figure out what it was, and Mom couldn't, either.

It started at about nine and went on till ten or later, and Dad was on his way to complain to the landlord, whose house was next door, when he decided instead to talk to Agnes Rath, who lived in the apartment under us.

It turned out that Agnes was scared sick.

When Dad knocked, she turned on her porch light and peeked out between her curtains, and, seeing that it was him, she opened her door and told him that Mr. Stink had been peeping in her window.

She'd seen him and, not knowing what to do, had turned off all her lights and crawled into the kitchen. Lying on the floor, she'd banged on the pipes under her sink as a signal.

So that was the clanking.

Agnes Rath's signal.

Well, a few nights later, a group of men ran through our yard and my dad ran with them, and then, not too long after that, fire leaped up on the hill around the spot where Mr. Stink had his shack, and nobody ever saw him again.

(Perhaps hurried footsteps and panting end in sounds of fire.)

Then Georgie Baxter got married, and moved into an apartment on the ground floor of the building next door to Jackie.

Georgie and his new wife, who everybody said was "a real looker," couldn't afford a long honeymoon. They got married on a Saturday, but, because Georgie had to work on Monday, they came back to their apartment Sunday night, and what awaited them was a shivaree.

People came from all directions, men, women, and kids, everybody carrying metal buckets or pots and beating on them with spoons to make a huge loud racket.

(Perhaps there is a background noise of banging pots and pans.)

Jackie and I were doing it like everybody else, beating away on pots with big spoons, though we had no idea why, all of us together creating this clamor as we closed in on the apartment building with Georgie and his new bride inside.

I stood with my pot and my spoon, beating away, whooping and feeling scared by the crazy noise we were making and the wild look in all the grownups' eyes, as if they were stealing or breaking something.

I wished more than anything that I knew why we were doing what we were doing.

About a week later, Jackie came and told me to hurry. At his house, he took me upstairs. It was Saturday, and he put his finger to his lips as he pulled me to the window and we looked down at Georgie and his new wife, in their bed without any clothes on, rolling and wrestling, and she looked like pudding or butter.

After a while, Jackie fell on the floor kind of moaning, like he had the time we went to the Orpheum Theatre to see the movie *Dracula*.

Perched way up high in the third balcony, we'd watched the ghost ship land in the mists with everyone dead, and, when Dracula swirled his cape and lay back in his coffin, Jackie got so scared he hid on the floor.

I looked down at him, and then back at the window, and the pudding woman saw me.

She glanced up, and, though I ducked as fast as I could, she caught me looking in her window.

If she told, what would happen?

Would I get run out of town like Mr. Stink?

If she told Georgie, or started banging on water pipes to alert people, would they come swarming and pounding on pots to surround me?

My fate was in the hands of Georgie Baxter's wife. What could be worse? Because she knew that I knew that under her clothes she was all pudding and bubbles.

It was a horrible worry, but I didn't tell anyone, not even Jackie.

That worry was mine alone, and it was maybe the worst worry, the worry to end all worries.

But then Jackie wandered into his kitchen one Saturday to find his stepmother, May, stuffing hunks of beef into the meat grinder. Her head swayed to music from the radio on the shelf above her, and her eyes were busy with something distant.

Jackie had gone into the kitchen because he was thirsty, so he stood on a chair to get a glass from the cupboard above the sink. He filled the glass to the brim from the faucet and drank every drop. The chair made a little squeal as he slid it back under the kitchen table.

That was when Stepmom May screamed.

Seeing the black hole of her mouth strung with saliva, Jackie was certain he had committed some unspeakable crime.

She raised a bloody mess toward him, her eyes icy and dead, and he knew that she was about to hurl a half-ground hunk of beef at him.

When instead she attacked the radio, yanking out the plug and circling her arm with the cord, he thought that she had gone insane.

It was only when she wailed "My thumb!" that he understood.

A hand crank powered the meat grinder, moving a gear that worked the teeth inside its cast-iron belly. With her right hand turning the crank, she'd used her left to stuff the meat into the mouthlike opening on top of the apparatus.

Her thumb had gone in too deep, and she'd failed to notice, or noticed only when she'd ground her thumb up with the beef. She ran out the door, the radio tied to her arm, rattling along behind her, and left him standing alone, blood dotting the worn-out ducks in the uneven linoleum, and the trickle of hope that had survived the loss of his real mom draining away.

When Jackie told me what had happened, as he did within minutes, it was as if I'd been there to see it, and I felt his deep, deep worry. It played on us like the spooky music in *Dracula*. It was strange and haunting and beyond anything we could explain, with our poor grasp of nouns and verbs.

And yet we knew that Jackie needed to try.

A downstairs door banged, and Jackie ran from where we stood on my porch, around the corner of the bannister, taking the steps two at a time until he landed in the yard.

Finding Agnes Rath, who nervously peered over her grocery bag at Jackie, he made his report: "Stepmom May cut her thumb off in the meat grinder!"

Suppertime was near, so people were coming and going.

Suddenly, he heard Red Weber approaching, followed by his wife.

Racing up to one and then the other, Jackie backtracked in the direction of their door so he could announce his dreadful news before they trampled him in their haste to get home: "Stepmom May cut her thumb off in the meat grinder!"

Henry Stoner, who lived beside us on the second floor, came around the corner, lunch bucket under his arm, and Jackie retreated up the stairs, never missing a step; he took corners, eluded rails. "Stuck it in and turned the crank!" he shrieked. "Stuck it in and turned the crank!"

Mrs. Stoner was home already, her shift at the plant having ended earlier than her husband's. She came out onto the porch and, in a gush of neighborly concern, prodded Jackie for more details.

"How is she?" Mrs. Stoner asked.

"Just ground it up!"

"Did you see it?"

But he could not budge from his point. The thing against which he had crashed clutched at him, like the tentacles of that monster squid we had all seen in *Wake of the Red Witch*. Now Jackie was being dragged down through inky confusion to some deep, lightless doom.

If he was ever to discover the cause of the terror endangering him and me and everyone he knew, as he believed, and I did, too, the search for an answer had to begin with what he'd seen. "Just stuck it in! And turned the crank, Mrs. Stoner! Just ground it up!"

"Can we do something for you, Jackie?"

Though he had time to look at her, he had time for nothing more. Mr. Hogan, who lived on the gravel road behind our house and who used our backyard as a shortcut home every night, was crossing.

Jackie hurtled down the stairs and jumped in front of Mr. Hogan, who was fleshy and soft and smelled of furniture polish.

Startled, Mr. Hogan took a step back. Before him stood a deranged-looking Jackie Rand. "Just stuck it in and ground it up!" he yelled.

"What?"

"Stepmom May cut her thumb off in the meat grinder! Stepmom May cut her thumb off in the meat grinder!"

"What?"

"Blood!" he shrieked. "Stuck it in and ground it off! Blood! Blood!"

Over the next hour, the four families in our building worked their way toward supper. Last-minute shopping was needed, and errands were run. Butter was borrowed from the second floor by the first floor, an onion traded for a potato. The odor of Spam mixed with beef, sauerkraut, wieners, and hash, while boiling potatoes sent out their steamy scent to mingle with that of corn and string beans, peas, coffee, baked potatoes, and pie.

All to the accompaniment of Jackie's "Blood!" and "Stepmom May!"

My mother, looking down over the bannister, said to my dad, "He looks so sad."

"Not to me."

"You don't think he looks sad?"

"Looks crazy, if you ask me. Nuttier than a pet coon, not that he doesn't always."

"Don't say that. Why would you say such a thing?"

My father went inside, leaving my mother alone. I felt invisible, perfectly forgotten, standing in the corner of the porch watching my mother witness Jackie's second encounter with Red Weber, who had returned from somewhere.

"Stepmom May! Stuck it in, Mr. Weber! Cut it off! Blood! Turned the crank! Stuck it in!"

Annoyed now, he brushed Jackie aside and snapped, "You told me! Now go home. Go home!"

Without a second's hesitation, my mother called down to invite Jackie up for dinner.

"Stepmom May," he said as he came in our door. "Turned the crank!" he addressed my dad. "Blood!" he delivered as he took a seat.

And, glowering at my baby sister in her high chair sucking milk from a bottle, he said, "Stepmom May cut her thumb off in the meat grinder!"

"Am I supposed to have my goddam supper with this fool and his tune?" my dad asked.

"Can't we talk about something else?" my mother said to Jackie.

Outside, a door slammed. Jackie could not rest. He bobbed in what might have been a bow. "Thanks for inviting me to dinner. It was real good."

He was gone, not having taken a bite, the screen door croaking on its hinges.

"Goddammit to hell," my dad said. "What does a person have to do to have his supper in peace around this nut factory!"

From afar, there was the rise and fall of Jackie's voice as he chased whomever he found: "Stepmom May! Cut her thumb off! Stuck it in and turned the crank!"

It was then that I understood. If Jackie understood, then or ever, I can't say. But the answer seemed simple and obvious once I saw it. If Stepmom May could do that to herself, what might she do to him? If she could lose track of the whereabouts of her own thumb, what chance did he have? What was he, after all, but a little boy, a small, mobile piece of meat? Certainly her connection to him was weaker than her connection to her own hand. Would he find himself tomorrow mistaken in her absentmindedness for a chicken, unclothed and basted in the oven? Must he be alert every second for her next blunder? Would he end up jammed into the Mixmaster, among the raisins and nuts?

What might any of our mothers do to any of us, we had to ask, given the strangeness of their love and their stranger neglect, those moments of distraction when they lost track of everything, even themselves, as they stared into worries that were all their own and bigger than anything we could hope to fathom?

I'm not sure how the word spread, but it did. We all heard it and knew to gather in the Haggertys' empty lot.

It was a narrow strip that ran down from the gravel road that separated the hill from the houses where we lived.

Nobody knew what the Haggertys planned to do with the lot. It wasn't wild, but it wasn't neat and cared for, either, and we all went there as soon as we could get out after supper.

We came from different directions and then we were there, nodding and knowing, but without knowing what we knew. For a while, we talked about Korea and the Chinese horde and the dangers that had our fathers leaning in close to their radios and cursing.

We got restless and somebody wanted to play Pump-Pump-Pullaway, but other people scoffed.

We tried Red Rover, and then Statue, where you got whirled around by somebody, and, when the boy who'd spun you yelled "Freeze!" as you stumbled around, you had to stop and stay that way without moving an inch, and then think of some kind of meaning for how you'd ended up.

We did that for a bit, but we all knew where we were headed.

Finally, somebody – it might have been me – said, "Let's play the blackout game."

The light had dimmed and the moon was now high, high enough that it was almost above us in the sky, with lots of stars, so we were ghostly and perfect.

Our mood had that something in it that made everyone feel as though this was what we had all been waiting for.

To play the blackout game, you'd stand with someone behind you, his arms around your chest, and you'd take deep breaths over and over, and the other boy would squeeze your chest until you passed out in a downpour of spangling lights.

The person behind you would then lay you down gently on your back in the grass, where you wandered around without yourself, until you woke up from a sleep whose content you'd never know.

We took turns. Jerry went, then Tommy and Butch. I went, and then Jackie was there, and he wanted to go.

Freddy Bird got behind Jackie, and Jackie huffed and huffed and sailed away, blacking out.

Freddy Bird let go and stepped clear.

Jackie toppled over backward. His butt landed and then his body slammed back, like a reverse jackknife, and, finally, his head hit with a loud crack.

A hurt look came over him, and a big sigh came out of his mouth: "Oh-h-h-h." More of a gasp, really, and he lay very still.

Motionless. Pale, I thought.

We all stared. He didn't move.

Freddy Bird was no longer pleased with how clever he was.

We waited for Jackie to wake up and he didn't. It seemed longer than usual.

"We didn't kill him, did we?"

"You don't die from that."

"It's because he's out twice. Once from the breathing stuff and once from banging his head."

We waited. Jackie didn't move.

I went closer.

Staring down, I had the crazy thought that Jackie Rand was like Jesus. Not that he was Jesus but that he was kind of our Jesus, getting the worst of everything for everybody, getting the worst that anybody could dish out, so that we could feel O.K. about our lives.

No matter how bad or unfair we might feel things were, they were worse for Jackie.

"Should we maybe tell somebody?"

A tiny tear appeared in the corner of each of Jackie's eyes.

He was the saddest person on earth, lying there, I thought.

The tears dribbled down his cheeks, and then his eyes blinked and opened and he saw where he was. His big pouty lips quivered.

He reached to rub the back of his head, and he started to cry really hard, and we knew that he was alive.

End of Play

THE BURNING SHIP
or
Suffocation Theory

THE BURNING SHIP, OR SUFFOCATION THEORY was first produced as a streaming film by Undermain Theatre (Katherine Owens, Founding Artistic Director; Bruce DuBose, Producing Artistic Director) in Dallas, TX, on April 8, 2021. The performance was directed by Jake Nice, with sets by Robert Winn, lighting by Steve Woods, and editing and photography direction by Marc Rouse. Bruce DuBose played the unnamed narrator.

THE BURNING SHIP was first published under the title "Suffocation Theory" in the October 12, 2020, issue of *The New Yorker*.

CHARACTER

OUR GUIDE – A man of a certain age and type, dressed in work clothes.

PRODUCTION NOTE

The script offers numerous possibilities for additions of projected images, offstage sound effect. The literal might work. For example: Distant gunfire. Crowd noises. The sounds of fire. Or it could be abstract sounds or music. There are times where the image could be of an animal when mentioned. There could be props. I'm writing this to indicate what might be a series of opportunities for a director and actor to explore. On the other hand, the piece might be best served by an expressive, versatile actor working on his own to render the material. I will make suggestions at a few places in the script where a prop or projection might be useful. But whatever is done, care must be taken not to encroach on the evocative reach of the actor and his material.

(A backdrop whose nature and color can be changed to seem like sky or perhaps some reflection of mood or emotion. Silence. Music: piano chords. A chair of some sort waits. A **MAN** of a certain age and type enters, taking off his coat. He walks to the chair, drops the coat and looks out.)*

Amanda surprised me when she said we had to move. I'd barely got in the door, barely been in the hallway of our apartment a second, when she passed in and out of my peripheral vision, catching sight of me, I guess, and making her announcement.

I'd been planning to take off my shoes and flop down on the couch with a cup of coffee to watch the news on TV – one blast of terrible news after another. I didn't know what the terrible news would be today, but I knew it'd be terrible.

Car crashes would be the least of it. Accidental ones, anyway. It's become common for people in cars to mow other people down. But that's not the only thing. There are terrorists and gun battles in shopping malls. Locals and tourists in Malaysia and Mali and London and Paris fleeing, stampeding, as soldiers duck behind jewelry displays and fast-food counters, hunting down militants in one boutique after another.

Bombs are often involved.

We've all become familiar with acronyms like I.E.D.

Long guns – that's another term we are necessarily familiar with.

---

* A license to produce *The Burning Ship* does not include a performance license for any third-party or copyrighted recordings. Licensees should create their own.

Boom, they go, these I.E.D.s, in churches, synagogues, mosques, concert halls, and the aforementioned shopping malls. Movie theatres, too. Strip malls. Scattered and maimed bodies, an outward gyre of victims propelled from the explosion.

Or the perpetrator (or perpetrators) might arrive with military-style weapons loaded with clips or magazines of hundreds of rounds.

Or like that goofy-looking white kid who went to a church meeting, where those prayerful African Americans welcomed him, and he listened to them read the Bible, and then he stood up and started shooting them.

Something is up. That's what I think. Something is up.

Anyway, back to the cars. Or maybe not. I don't want to forget the pundits, who come on right after the shootings or the bombings, as regular as clockwork, these experts, talking heads, network contributors on national security or terrorism or profiling the criminal mind. Lone wolf or affiliated? A bomb goes off and these experts weigh in, a banner below them broadcasting their names and specialties. I find the fact that they show up consoling, the way they chart a course through the mayhem. Anyway, I came in the door eager to get settled in front of the terrible news. I'd grown addicted, you might say. "Dependent" was probably closer. I had come to feel that it was important for me to pay attention to it all. It seemed the responsible thing to do.

A gun, a bomb, or a car, the instrument was always in the hands of a person or people overcome by the power of this very powerful idea, this irresistible idea – at least to them – that killing a bunch of strangers would solve whatever problem they thought they couldn't solve in any other way. The problem might be personal – a lost job, a failed marriage. Or it might be cosmic, with supernatural imperatives. Some astrophysical battle between light and dark. This religion or that one. Or this one over that one. But the solution was always the same.

Dead strangers.

Sometimes these terrible news events were deemed to be terrorist events – bloodshed with a political motive. Sometimes the deaths were the result of rage or simple insanity. Not that the factors couldn't be combined. And then there were storms, floods, tornadoes. Those received some attention, too. Entire small towns wiped out. Overturned double-wides.

That kind of thing.

But I have to say that bad weather was a relief when compared with all the other pieces of terrible news, because it didn't have a human behind it. Unless it was due to our ignorance, greed, indifference, self-delusion. Everybody argued, "Climate change this and that."

But not this one environmentalist.

With dark, stricken eyes, he said that calling it "climate change" was wrong, because it should be called "climate suffocation." That was what would happen once the oceans stopped making oxygen, which was already happening, with dead zones and oxygen declines. The oceans were suffocating. And after they stopped producing oxygen the trees would stop, too. And the fish and sea life would suffocate; the animals would all suffocate.

When I caught up with Amanda, I told her that I liked our apartment. I hadn't known we were thinking of moving. But she had everything arranged, she said. The movers were on their way up. I went to the window and there were cars and people on the street, but no moving van.

Then I heard loud knocking, and she yelled at me to "let them in," and when I failed to move, pretending I was captivated by things outside, she ran past me, shouting that she didn't understand why she had to do everything.

I said I didn't know why, either.

They came in, six big men in uniforms, with their names embroidered on their shirts in red stitching, right above the chest pocket – Brett and Tom and Buck were three of the names. Actually, it was seven men. And when I counted again there were eight. There was a logo of a truck on the back of their jackets. They were laughing and pushing one another, like cowboys or football players. They started taking our furniture – two of them to the armchair, three to the couch. Several were dismantling the television.

Grabbing my shoes before one of the movers took them, I headed for the door.

The new apartment was a big disappointment. Too small to be a real warehouse, it had that feeling of vast emptiness one finds in a warehouse.

Amanda kept saying that it was perfect. She ran from room to room, shouting, "I like it! I like it! It's perfect!"

I still didn't understand why we'd had to leave our old place. I really didn't like the new neighborhood.

And we had this new roommate.

I could tell the minute I saw him that I disliked him and he disliked me. Amanda said that we'd get used to each other. She said that it would work out and that it would save money. We'd been living frugally but nicely, I thought. Money didn't seem to be a problem. At least, not more of a problem than it was for most middle-of-the-road people. So I was completely confused by what she said. I could tell that the kids were unhappy, too, wandering about barefoot, in clothes that needed to be washed.

I told Amanda that I didn't like the new apartment or the new neighborhood. She gave me her patented fed-up headshake, which left no doubt that I'd just confirmed something she knew about me and could barely tolerate.

The point here was that, although the new neighborhood wasn't that far from the old one, it was drastically different. Our old place was on a wide, beautiful street running along the crest of a hill. Below it was another street running parallel to the crest of the hill. And below that another parallel street, and so on, for five streets down, each one getting narrower, more potholed, and dirtier.

Desolate and chaotic would be a good way to evoke the lonely, abandoned mood of the last street, the fifth street, where the new apartment was.

Almost no one had a car and nearly everyone you saw was bedraggled and despondent. The amount of trash adrift in the wind and kicked by these dispirited people steadily grew. It wasn't a class system, Amanda said, but just the way things were.

I'd gone out to look around and get a better feel for the new neighborhood when it suddenly got dark, and there were no street lights. I was on one of the side streets that ran up and down the hill. It was an irritating feature of the area that the street signs disappeared as you got lower. I couldn't remember how to get back into the new building. The door in front of me didn't look right, but I went in anyway, and started to climb the stairs. Usually, in this type of building, there's a door on each landing, marked with a number to indicate the floor. But this stairway didn't offer that kind of exit or information; nor did it switch back the way most stairways do. It just kept going straight up, which meant that the building was very, very tall, and unusually wide.

At last, I spied a door very far above me, a hundred yards or more. It seemed too far to go without knowing if I was in the right place.

After backing down a few steps, I turned and hurried the rest of the way until I was outside, where I recognized the shabby façade of our building across the street. I didn't have a key to the front entrance yet, but one of the movers held the door open for me.

The new roommate was the first person I saw when I got to the apartment. Blond, younger than me, muscular across the shoulders, which was all I could see of him, except for his calves and the lower portion of his thighs, he trailed water on the floor, his hair sopping. He had wrapped a beach towel around himself and tucked it high under his armpits, the way women do, so the towel covered him from his armpits to his thighs. In one hand, he held a sandwich that looked like ham and cheese on white bread, gobs of mustard dripping out, and in his other hand he had a pistol, and he was walking around the way people do when they're looking for something. "Did you lose something?" I asked.

"Why?"

"You look like you're looking for something."

"No."

"Where'd you get that?" I nodded in the general direction of his hand and fixed my eyes on the gun.

"It's mine," he told me. "Don't worry."

"I don't want guns in this place."

"It's just one."

"I'll get one, too. If you have one, I think I'd better have one."

"If you want."

"That's what I'll do."

"So right now the one I have is the only one here." He smiled icily.

"But I'm going to get one."

He pointed the pistol at me. It was silver-plated with a long barrel and a white pearl handle. "Don't do that."

"Why?"

"I don't like it."

"Why?"

He put the gun against my temple. Then he pressed the barrel into my cheek. He stuck it against my stomach and my chest. He bumped my cheek with the tiny tip thing on the end of the barrel – one, two, three, four, five, too many times. He tried to poke it into my mouth. I pushed it away. "I don't like it here," I said.

"I do. It's nice."

"I don't like the neighborhood."

I don't know how long we talked like that. Amanda came back from wherever she was, and I said I needed to take a shower. She pointed me to the bathroom, and that was when I discovered that there was no shower. Just this old bathtub full of scummy water, which must have been left from the new roommate's bath. There was rust on the faucet handles, and the tub had old-fashioned legs, like chicken legs.

I started shouting that I needed a bathroom with a shower. We argued for a while. Amanda looked hurt and angry, but she kept yelling, so I kept yelling. I don't know for how long. But when we stopped the President was on the television, shouting.

He wanted revenge. He wanted to get even. He started reading from a list of names of people and countries that he liked. He had a second list of people and countries that he hated, and it was long, and eventually some of the names from the first list started showing up.

Then the front-door buzzer buzzed, indicating that somebody wanted to be let in, and when I went down and pulled the door open there was Amanda, with dirt smeared on her face and a thick black hose thing in her hands.

"I got this for you," she said.

At that instant, I heard cursing. A large, lumpy man in a ripped shirt jumped out of his car and threw open the hood. "It's gone, goddammit!"

I looked for Amanda, but didn't see her. Something tugged at my pants leg. She was down on her belly, and I realized that the dirty tube thing was a car part that she had stolen. "For the shower," she said.

"What?"

"For your shower." That was her way of saying that she'd taken the hose because I'd been upset. She explained that she hoped to rig a shower by running the car hose from the tub faucet up over this kind of towel-rack thing sticking out of the wall, so the water could pour down.

"But it will be filthy, because it's a car part," I told her. "You have not really thought this through."

"No. The water will clean it out." She looked scared, and I wanted to help her, although I was mad. I inched the hose in through the doorway, so as not to draw attention from the owner, who stomped around his car, screaming and slamming the hood. I'd barely shut the door, with both of us safely inside, when my cell phone dinged.

It was a text from PETA: Friend – we have heartbreaking news: Slow lorises are threatened with extinction. But, instead of being protected, they are trafficked, because people want these cuddly creatures for pets or as status symbols.

A photograph presented a tiny primate, its furry face contorted by a yearning to be friends with everyone.

> *(Perhaps a slow loris is projected on the backdrop. For a moment the man gazes up at it. And then he turns out and continues.)*

Amanda and I were reading to the kids. It was a children's book, and we all four nestled around the open pages with their energetic illustrations. A man came in. Sports coat, linen slacks, top three buttons of his shirt undone. He carried a bottle of wine. For an instant, I didn't remember that we had a new roommate, but, even when I did, I had to ask what he was doing.

He shook his head and complained about his inability to find a corkscrew. What the hell did he have to do to get along in this place?

The children were waiting for the story to continue.

Amanda watched the new roommate, her eyes full of concern.

And then I remembered. They were having an affair. Amanda and Reed. How had I ever forgotten? It had been going on for a long time.

He was over by the window looking out. His baggy trousers had baggy pockets, and there were other pockets in his coat. His pistol could have been in any one of them, and I didn't know which, but I did know that it wasn't in his hand.

I sprang on him and got him in a choke hold from behind. He wanted to grab for his pistol, wherever it was, but he couldn't make his hands do anything but fly up to claw at my forearm, which I'd locked around his throat. He was gurgling with a kind of pleading sound that might have been his attempt to say "Please" and "Don't" and "Stop."

I constricted every muscle I had, so that he'd never get away. I could feel the life going out of him, and I could see the light in his eyes dimming in the full-length mirror that Amanda held up. He was too heavy for me to keep upright, so we sank to the floor, where his life continued to slip out of him.

Amanda said, "What are you doing? Let him go."

I asked myself if I dared to do as she wanted. Or did I really want him dead? He would be my bitter enemy for as long as we lived now that I'd done this.

I wished Amanda weren't holding the mirror, because then I wouldn't have to see his eyes. They were so lonely and hopeless. But she made sure I saw.

I collapsed off him. He flopped onto his back. Amanda hurried to him. She brushed his brow tenderly and placed her mouth over his. She pinched his nose shut and blew into his mouth, and I knew I'd made two terrible mistakes – one in attacking him and another in letting him go. She peeked at me out of narrow, hate-filled eyes as she established a rhythm for puffing the life back into him, until he let out a growling cough full of tears and then curled into a fetal position.

After a minute, she helped him to his feet and they went off.

I'm not sure where the young woman came from. She might have come from another apartment, or from one of the many rooms in the new apartment that I hadn't been able to look into yet. She was animated, talking to people I didn't know, who I assumed were Amanda's friends, or maybe the new roommate's. There was a circle of four or five men and three women, and they talked excitedly to the young woman. They were fascinated by her, though I could tell they didn't know why. And then she reached for some chips in a bowl. As she ate, her eyes came to rest on me.

She didn't say a word, just crossed over to where I sat in an armchair and lowered herself onto my lap. She took my hands and put them on her waist. I didn't care if people stared at us. An elderly man in a vest and bow tie approached with a tray of party snacks. She asked for a glass of water and rocked her hips a little forward and back, causing a shiver in me, and then in her.

"Where did you come from?" I asked her, thinking I'd make idle conversation.

"Troy." Her dark eyes had a fathomless quality, with flickering light in the irises.

My cell phone dinged, and, though I didn't recognize the organization that was texting, I did see what it wanted to tell me: "Rabbits are screaming."

I said, "Troy? Really? The city?"

"Troy. Yes."

"The ancient city?" I imagined her ship at anchor outside, where the dirty street contended with wind and debris, its square sail furled, its oars pointed skyward.

It was dark now and some men were gathered at a table in a little room off the kitchen. They were bunched around a light, and the biggest of them glowered at me. I didn't recognize him, or any of them, but when I got closer I saw the smallish television that entranced them, their bodies warped by their angry, worried concentration.

The volume was low, but I heard two sombre voices, before I saw the team of male and female newscasters.

"The President is unhappy," the sharp-faced female anchor said.

The men at the table conferred in intense tones. "The president is unhappy," read the crawl across the bottom of the screen.

"He imagines himself happy," the male anchor declared. "He imagines himself young. He imagines himself handsome. He imagines he is well-liked by everyone in the world. He imagines he is omnipotent."

"Day after day," the woman said, her lucidly intelligent eyes blinking. She had straight brown hair. "Night after night. Prowling the halls."

The men at the table were solemn, nodding at the screen and then at me in a uniform way that made me uneasy.

Duppedee-do! went my phone, delivering an e-mail with a yellow Labrador and a golden retriever looking at me mournfully, each trapped in a structure of metal rods that immobilized its head, as text explained, "These innocent dogs await the pharmaceutical experimenters who will drill holes in their skulls, in order to inject a deadly virus into their brains to kill them slowly."

"We're trying to help the President," one of the men said to me. "He needs our help. No one understands him. He wants people to understand him so that they'll like him. So we're trying to understand him, and then like him, so we can teach everybody how to understand him and like him."

"Oh," I said.

The man who was talking turned away, and so did the others, except for one who stared me down, his spiteful eyes full of plans. Suspicion clouded the air between us, like an oil spill.

I went off down the hall and in a door. Amanda and the new roommate were in bed. Just lying on their backs with their eyes open. They seemed to be staring at the ceiling. "What do you want?" he said.

"Nothing," Amanda answered.

"Not you." He poked her. "Him."

"Who?"

"Him."

I left.

Behind me, Amanda kept saying, "Who? Who?"

"Open your eyes, Amanda. For God's sake, open your eyes – he was just here."

Sinister men were waiting for me. They wore dark suits. They circled me and then moved closer. "You're in danger," one of them whispered. His eyes shimmered, like broken glass. "I know," I told him.

"We want to help you."

"We want to warn you," a different one said. He shoved me.

"We want to protect you," the first one said, and he shoved me harder. I staggered back a few steps.

"Don't trip," another one said.

"There's a border," one said. They kept shoving me every time they said something. "There's a border that is a boundary."

"Don't cross it."

"It's a boundary that is a border."

"I understand," I said. "Now let me alone."

"We're done anyway." They tried to speak in unison, creating noise like an out-of-kilter engine ready to explode.

I went toward the television I heard blasting. Not the little one in the room off the kitchen but the big one that I usually watched. The little one was gone. The men who'd huddled around it must have taken it. It seemed they'd taken the room, too. The kitchen was there, but the small room off the kitchen was gone.

Duppedee-do! went my phone: "Help. It's up to you." I hit Delete and walked away.

I didn't know where I was going. When my phone dinged again, I knew better than to look, but I did anyway, and I learned that a man, infuriated by his crying infant daughter, had stuck his finger down her throat to make her be quiet.

I kept walking. I don't know for how long I walked and walked, but I came to the small room off the kitchen. It was back, as were the little television and the men watching it. A beaming, impish man identified as a Presidential adviser announced, "The President knows more than anyone about everything."

The interviewer, a woman with a quirky mouth, asked, "More than the scientists, who –"

"Absolutely."

"You're saying he knows more than the scientists, who –"

"Yes, yes."

"Wait. I'm speaking of people who are experts in their particular field, such as climate change. Let's talk about that."

"Cassandras. All of them."

"Cassandras? Your position is that the experts on the Intergovernmental Panel on Climate Change are Cassandras? That those predicting disappearing glaciers, rising sea levels, and –"

"Cassandras, Cassandras, Cassandras."

"But she was a prophetess. You know. She told the future."

"Exactly." His face formed a childish, doll-like grin, while his eyes disclosed cold-blooded desires that he believed no one could see. "A prophetess people didn't listen to. If you're a Cassandra, nobody listens to you. That's the great part, that's the fun part, the thrilling part – they know the future, and they tell us, but we don't have to listen, because the President is smarter than anyone."

Duppedee-do! went my phone: "Australia is on fire!"

Images flashed: The sky blazing with supercharged pillars of twisting flame. People retreating to a beach. A woman spraying water onto frightened alpacas, their long necks pivoting between her and the burning world.

Amanda and the new roommate were throwing my things around. Into boxes. Into piles on the floor. I didn't know what was going on. When I first came upon them, I was too startled to speak. I stood off to the side, hoping they'd explain without my needing to ask, but they just kept throwing my things. Finally, he looked at me, clearly thinking I was the stupidest person he'd ever seen in his life. "Amanda," he said.

"Oh, I know, he's utterly useless." She looked at me. "You're in the way." And then, to him, she said, "Don't pay any attention to him."

I couldn't take it. I shouted, "What are you doing?"

"We're throwing all this junk away," she said.

"Those are mine," I said.

"It's all junk."

"I want it. I like it."

They laughed. "We're getting new things," they said, one after the other.

I picked up a short-sleeved shirt. "This is a good thing." I grabbed a coffee cup. "I really like this. I've had it all my life."

They laughed so hard they started to gasp. "He likes it. He likes it. We're getting rid of it. All of it. It's old."

"Her, too," one of them said.

"What?"

"Her, too," the other one said.

And I realized that they were talking about my mother, who I remembered was in a room at the very end of the hallway, a little room you reached after almost doubling back. I'd hidden her there so they wouldn't know, but they must have found her.

"No," I said. "You will not!" I hurried toward the hallway, aware that they were laughing uproariously behind me.

"We've already done it," they shouted. "She's gone."

It was maybe the worst laughter I'd ever heard. This was what they'd been thinking about when they were in bed, looking at the ceiling, and I walked in.

"We can keep the reading lamp," I said, rushing back. "I think the reading lamp and some books."

"No, it's all going."

"We're moving," he said, and she said it, too.

"But we just got here!"

"No, no, not you."

"You're not moving. We are."

The moving men walked by with their stitched names, all nine of them, going into a room and shutting the door. I saw how big their feet were. "If you're moving," I said, "if you're –"

"That's right."

"Why take my things? I like them."

"I hate them."

"Amanda hates them."

"But they're mine. And you're moving out."

"You're such an idiot," Amanda said. "You don't understand anything."

"Just leave my things, goddammit!" I screamed.

She ran in, the young woman. She searched wildly, perspiration on her brow. She had something to tell me, and her mouth was open with fear that she was too late.

Other people walked and talked all through the apartment. It was a party of some kind. Amanda and the roommate laughed, welcoming their guests. They were hosting.

When Amanda gestured at me, the guests regarded me with the dismissive, intolerant attitude she modelled for them. The party guests shouted, drinking rabidly, grabbing goblets off trays.

The young woman disappeared in the ribaldry, everyone smelling of perfume and drowning one another out in their hysterical good time.

"It's a housewarming. In reverse," Amanda said. And the way she howled, and everyone howled with her, made it clear that this was the wittiest comment ever made by the wittiest woman ever to live. "The end is here," she added. "The absolute end."

"Of everything," the new roommate said.

They howled even louder.

The young woman whirled back into view. Several men jumped in front of her. They grabbed at her arm.

The women stayed aloof, behind blinding veneers of gems and furs, jewelry storming their ears, hair, and necks.

But the young woman escaped. It seemed impossible, but she did it, and she came straight to where I sat in the big armchair.

Her eyes affirmed that, as I'd thought, she did have something to tell me. Out of breath from wrestling free from the party guests, she sank onto my lap, and leaned close, whispering so softly I didn't understand. "What?" I asked. "What did you say?"

She threw her head back in a way that suggested anguish.

"Mankind is suicidal, I'm afraid – a suicidal species."

"Is that what you said?"

"I thought you heard me."

"Oh, I hope that's not true. It's just too hopeless to think that. I want to have a little hope."

"But what if there isn't any?"

I stared into her profound eyes, following their dark invitation to consider her wide forehead, her high cheekbones, the depths she had yet to reveal. "Troy?" I said. "That's where Cassandra lived, isn't it?"

"Yes. I am Cassandra, the prophetess, whom no one believes. Cassandra, full of mourning and prophecy." Like the horizon, her eyes went on, until they could go no further.

I was so relaxed, so dreamy, she could have said anything.

"It's your body," she said. "And my body. We're animals. Two animals."

I just wanted her to keep moving, and letting me fill with that bewildering syrup for which I felt only love and gratitude.

"Are you Cassandra? Are you really?" I wanted to hear her say it again, but I couldn't wait for her to respond. "I like to think that people are good at heart, Cassandra."

"We all do, but unfortunately they're not anything at heart."

She closed her eyes and chanted, "Thus said the hawk to the nightingale with speckled neck, while he carried her high up among the clouds, gripped fast in his crooked talons, and she cried pitifully. To her, he spoke disdainfully: 'Miserable thing, why do you cry out? One far stronger than you now holds you fast, and you must go wherever I take you, Songstress. And, if I please, I will make my meal of you, or let you go. He is a fool who tries to withstand the stronger, for he does not gain mastery and suffers pain in addition to his shame.'"

For a second of enigmatic sorrow she paused before explaining, "So said Hesiod, the Greek, of the fast-flying hawk, the long-winged bird."

I groped to keep my hands on her waist. "Doesn't it make you sad?"

"That people are not good at heart? Of course it does."

"No, no. That no one believes you."

"It's a curse." Again, she closed her eyes. "We possess in full bounty all that animals need to live, any animal, all animals. Of which man is one. Except he has decided that he isn't."

"Because mankind has a spirit," shouted one of the partygoers celebrating the end of everything. Amanda handed him a megaphone, as if she were dissatisfied with how loud he'd been so far.

"Mankind may or may not have a spirit," Cassandra roared. "But, either way, our bodies are animals and that's true of me, you, Amanda, and the hawk."

"Oh, Cassandra," I said. "Why are you doing this?"

"Bodies," she sighed, and shivered. "They want things. We're so ignorant, and we hate being ignorant, and we hate being told we are ignorant. But we hate most of all being told we are animals. Especially when we are tall men, or short men, or fat men, or balding men, or gray-haired men in suits who believe that we eat, shit, and breathe money, and so we don't need food, water, or air. Here is my prophecy: Breath after breath, the air insults us by saving us, by letting us live a few seconds more. But only a few, before another breath is needed. Twenty-three thousand and forty times a day."

Her lips exhaled her vision: "I am Cassandra and this is my prophecy. To prove that we are not animals, that we are above and superior to animals, we will destroy everything that an animal needs to live, and thus obliterate our world and ourselves."

Color and light shift inside me. I'm a landscape before a storm. I've assumed that all those men and women with their guns, cars, and bombs – I've assumed that they don't really solve their problems. That the solution of dead strangers doesn't work. But what if it does? What if the mayhem they cause, the bloodshed and slaughter, in fact solves their problems, and could also solve mine? They don't know until the last minute. I can know only at my last minute.

I begin to feel it.

Holding the long gun. Watching the world flee before me, the blood on the pavement, the raining flecks of gore. I'll never know unless I try.

It's happening already, just by thinking, just by considering, a strange but powerful sense of completion. There are gun shops not far from here. I'll go to one. I'll tell no one. I'll go about everything as I always have, quietly, privately.

It seems obvious now. Dead strangers solve everything. "Mankind is a suicidal species." The evidence is in. And, so, what could it matter, even if I'm wrong, and the problems remain, and the only thing that's gone is a few strangers and me?

I make excuses to Amanda and the new roommate about my travels. I tell them that since they are thinking of moving I am thinking of moving, too.

The way they smirk and roll their eyes tells me how much they underestimate me. I imagine Amanda's shock when I shoot her. I'll start with them. Him first, one in the chest and one in the head, before he can move to get his pistol. Then her.

I'll go on from them to strangers. To the fat men in suits, the balding, or gray-haired, or sleek-bodied men. But first Amanda and the new roommate.

"I'm not moving again," I'll scream. "Where did you put my mother?"

I start evaluating fat men on the street. I need to pick the right fat man to make it worthwhile, and there are so many of them. Maybe a bald man. But there are lots of them, too.

In a nearby state, I find a gun show in a defunct supermarket with "GONE OUT OF BUSINESS" painted in white on its windows.

The inside is an expanse of arid deadness, where I wander about, hoping to blend in with the men and women in sneakers and boots, T-shirts and jeans, sports coats and camo clothing. They munch chips and hot dogs, gulp soda and coffee, looking awestruck as they shoulder a weapon and peer down the sight.

(Perhaps he picks up a weapon.)

Driving home with an AK-47, a twelve-gauge shotgun, and ammo for both, I begin to worry that I might have betrayed my intentions somehow.

Churning anxiety advises me to act more swiftly than I was thinking.

(Perhaps he starts loading the weapon.)

At the apartment, Amanda and the new roommate pass me in the hall, smug and dismissive. I start to think that it may not matter which fat man I shoot. It's probably not a matter of getting the right one. Any fat man, or balding man, in a suit. Or maybe not in a suit. Or maybe not even a fat man or a balding man, but just someone.

But then I wake up in the dark, knowing that my Dear One is dying. I feel stricken and alone with the force of this knowing. I want to escape it, but it takes me into the blackest of nights. I'd forgotten her, and now she is dying and she's looking for me to say goodbye.

How could I have forgotten her? My Dear One, my Dear One.

She's down by the sea. She's standing at a harbor, or a dock, or a port, or a waterfront at the edge of dark water, and she's looking off into the dark water.

For an instant, I think she's Cassandra. But I know I'm only thinking this because I want to understand more than I can.

She's older and deeper and more loving than Cassandra. My Dear One is everything to me, and I want to say goodbye to her, too. I want to tell her that I love her. I have always loved her.

I start down toward her, because the gigantic lightless vessel coming to carry her off is crashing close through the waves. I'm sorry I forgot her, and I have to get to her before she is gone. I'm running, but trying to conserve energy, because I don't know how long it will take before I reach her.

Strangers start coming from the opposite direction. They don't mean to block the way, and yet they do, because they're frightened, and their fear makes them clumsy.

First a bearded man, and then a trio of men and a gaggle of women, panting as they go up the hill I need to go down. Some carry babies or drag children. I dodge and shove to get through them, but it's almost impossible, and I realize from the wild look in their eyes that they are almost blind with fear.

Suddenly someone pushes me out of the way, wanting to get past me.

He's shouting for my Dear One, trying to get to her, too. He announces that he's near, begging her to answer if she hears him. He's taller than me, with unnaturally thin, expressive arms and legs. He's graceful, and his voice is cultured.

He shoves people aside, and, through the jumbled bodies climbing toward me, I see him reach her and take her in his arms.

She's slight, a wisp, looking up at him, but so precious. He loves her, he tells her. He is shameless in his passion, pointing to the sky to invoke it as his witness. He has come to say goodbye and she must know that he loves her more than anything or anyone else on earth ever could.

I have to turn back. I cannot go to my Dear One now and say the things I want to say, because he has said them all. My words will ring hollow and insincere, like I'm imitating him.

I join the rabble laboring up the hill, and now that I am in their ranks I understand that they are fleeing the dark water below, where burning boats inflame the rolling waves and the sky, as far as anyone can see.

Men and women flow on, lugging boxes, bags, and children, the sound of their breath like a growing wind.

When I nearly stumble over something, I look down at one of the big fat men, who has fallen, his suit in tatters. The wheels of a cart grind over an old woman who barely responds.

And then I hear my Dear One behind me.

I see her fighting to reach me. She calls to me that she wants me.

When my Dear One reaches me, we both start to cry. She says that she had to find me. She could not go out onto the dark sea without telling me she loved me. Without saying goodbye. She must say goodbye to me.

All the things I wanted to say to her she wants to say to me. As I hold her, she is as slight as when I first saw her, barely there in her clothing.

People bang against us, and then part to go by, sweeping on in two streams that rejoin in one ongoing throng.

After a while, we begin to walk with them, and we are refugees, too.

End of Play

Milton Keynes UK
Ingram Content Group UK Ltd.
UKHW030704120324
439302UK00017B/1044